NEW GIRL

Phoenix Lovegrove

COPYRIGHT

This work is a work of fiction. Names, characters, businesses, organisations, places, events, and incidents are either the products of the author's imagination or used in a fictitious manner. Any resemblance to actual persons, living or dead, or actual events is purely coincidental.

No part of this publication may be reproduced, distributed, or transmitted in any form or by any means, including photocopying, recording, or other electronic or mechanical methods, without the prior written permission of the Author or the Publisher, except in the case of brief quotations embodied in critical reviews and certain other non-commercial uses permitted by copyright law.

For permission requests, email the Author / Publisher on the address below:

Email: info@neuvare.com

Author page: www.phoenixlovegrove.neuvare.com

Publisher Website: www.neuvare.com

Book Cover by Neuvare

First edition: 2024

SHARE YOUR EXPERIENCE

Dear Esteemed Reader,

I am thrilled to extend my deepest gratitude to you for selecting my book from the vast array of options available. Your decision to embark on this literary journey fills my heart with profound appreciation and excitement.

As you immerse yourself in the pages of this book, I hope you find yourself transported into the world I've crafted, drawn to the characters, and engaged by the unfolding narrative. Your experience as a reader is invaluable, and I would be honoured if you could spare a moment to share your thoughts.

Reviews serve as the lifeblood of any writer's career. They offer not only invaluable feedback but also guide other readers in discovering this book amidst the multitude of options available. Whether you choose to share a brief sentiment or provide a detailed analysis, your honest opinion holds immeasurable significance.

If the book resonates with you, I kindly invite you to consider leaving a review on the platform where you acquired or encountered this book. Your support in spreading the word would be immensely appreciated.

Conversely, if the book did not meet your expectations, I welcome your constructive criticism. Such feedback enables me to evolve and improve as a writer, ensuring that future works better align with the desires of my readers.

Once again, I extend my sincerest gratitude for your time, attention, and willingness to embark on this literary voyage with me. Your support fuels my passion for storytelling, and I am deeply grateful for each reader who joins me on this adventure.

Warm regards,

Phoenix Lovegrove

Author of New Girl

TABLE OF CONTENTS

CHAPTER ONE

New Beginnings

WITH A RESIGNED sigh, Ava sealed the last of her bulging suitcases with a decisive zip. Clasping the handle of her overstuffed suitcase with her right hand and her boarding pass in the other. She cast a lingering gaze around her childhood bedroom. Once adorned with faded surfer posters and an array of shells gathered from the beach, the walls now stood bare. Etched within those four walls were countless memories. Taking a deep breath, Ava felt an irresistible urge to capture the familiar salty breeze drifting in through the window, a sensory memento before it vanished from her life.

Her father had been transferred to another office out of state. In less than 12 hours, they would bid farewell to the sun-kissed shores of San Diego, embarking on a journey spanning over 2,500 miles toward the heart of Michigan. The sway of her father's professional responsibilities held the reins to her destiny, orchestrating the path she was destined to tread.

A cocktail of nerves and excitement churned in Ava's stomach. Although she desired a location with varying seasons, the thought of leaving this sun-filled paradise was too daunting for her to put into words. There was a latent fear that she might lose herself outside the comforting cadence of the ocean's lullabies, which for so long, had cradled her to sleep each night.

How was this spirited tomboy going to adapt to a complete transformation, trading her tank tops and flip-flops for the bulk of winter jackets and the sturdiness of snow boots? The transition promised more than just a change in wardrobe; it hinted at a shift in lifestyle, a metamorphosis from carefree summer days to the challenges and wonders of the winter season.

She was exchanging those leisurely strolls under the warm rays of the sun for snow-laden streets, distinguished by the crunch of frost beneath her boots. The familiar sensation of the sun's rays kissing her skin was about to be replaced by the crisp bite of winter air, tingling against her cheeks, sending shivers down her spine.

Ava stole a last glimpse of the downtown skyline glittering beyond her bedroom window. They were exchanging the ritual of waking up to golden beach sunrises for the stark, grey dawns of the Midwest? In less than 24 hours, the answer would unfold, revealing how adept this California-born girl could be beyond the cocoon of familiarity.

The impending dawn heralded a reckoning for Ava as she pondered her adaptability in a new school within the unfiltered reality of the outside world. Even as the act of departure gripped her heart like a vice, beneath the swirling apprehension, a spark of excitement kindled. Ava was on the cusp of a new adventure, set to unfold on a distant horizon.

This juncture was a litmus test, challenging Ava to discover if she possessed the resilience to thrive in unfamiliar terrain. The threads of nostalgia, woven into the fabric of her childhood room, were being unravelled, making way for the uncharted chapters of her life. As she closed the door behind her, Ava carried with her not only the weight of poignant farewells but also the anticipation of the myriad possibilities that awaited her in the vast expanse of the world beyond.

CHAPTER TWO

Sophomore Year

IT WAS THE first day of sophomore year, and I was running late as usual. I rushed into Mr Jensen's history class just as the bell rang, quickly scanning the room for a seat. The only one left was next to some girl I didn't recognise. She must be new, I thought. As Mr Jensen began the lesson, I quietly slid into the desk beside her.

"Good morning, class, My name is Mr Jensen, and I will be your history teacher for the year," he said cheerfully. "Let's start by introducing ourselves. Starting with the back row, let's move from left to right. Please share with the class your name and an interesting fact about yourself."

I internally groaned as I disliked these icebreaker introductions.

Most people's 'interesting facts' were pretty boring... plays football, just got back from vacation, loves pizza. Finally, it was the new girl's turn.

"Hi, I'm Ava. I just moved here last week from San Diego," she said simply. A few kids murmured hello.

"And your interesting fact?" prompted Mr Jensen.

"Well, I surf competitively back in California. And I have a pet pig named Bacon Bits," Ava replied nonchalantly. Okay, now she had everyone's attention. A competitive surfer girl with a pet pig? You didn't see that every day in suburban Michigan.

"Well, aloha and welcome, Ava. We're happy to have you here," Mr Jensen grinned. Ava gave a small smile, then looked down at her notebook.

I spent the rest of class stealing curious glances at the new girl. She was undeniably pretty with long honey-blonde hair, sun-kissed skin, and eyes the colour of sea glass. But she also seemed quiet and guarded. I wondered what had brought her all the way from California.

The bell rang, and everyone gathered up their things to leave. As I stood up, Ava dropped one of her notebooks.

"Here, let me grab that for you," I said, quickly stooping to pick it up.

"Thanks," she replied, tucking a stray strand of blond hair behind her ear. "I'm Ava. And you are...?"

"I am Andrea, but people call me Andi. That's Andi with an i," I replied. "So, California huh. That must have been pretty nice. What brings you to small-town Michigan?"

Ava shrugged. "My dad got transferred here for work. I miss the ocean though."

I glanced down and noticed a small surfer girl pendant around her neck. "Well, we've got the Great Lakes at least. Not quite the Pacific, but hey, water's water."

She appeared taken aback. "Wait, you telling me that people really surf in this area?"

"See for yourself!" I responded. "I could show you one of the local spots this weekend if you're interested in checking it out."

A smile spread across Ava's face, making her sea-glass eyes sparkle. "I'd love that!"

"Cool, it's a date then," I grinned. Oh god… did I just say date? Smooth, Andrea. Real smooth. I felt my cheeks flush red. Thankfully, Ava didn't seem to notice my awkward phrasing.

"Looking forward to seeing you this weekend," she exclaimed cheerfully, waving goodbye as she made her way to her next class. I watched as her ponytail swayed from side to side until she disappeared into the crowd.

As I turned to make my way to my next class, I suddenly veered off to the right to avoid bumping into someone. To my surprise, I came face to face with my good friend Mateo instead. He raised his eyebrows at me playfully.

"Soo… you and the new girl, huh?"

I playfully punched his arm. "Dude, I just met her. I was only being nice."

"Uh-huh, sure," Mateo smirked. "Given your reputation, it's likely that you'll become completely enthralled by her within a month."

"You're delusional," I scoffed, trying to act casual. But secretly, I wondered if Mateo was right. There was just something intriguing about Ava that I couldn't quite put my finger on. One thing was for sure, this was going to be an interesting year.

That Saturday, I drove Ava out to the shores of Lake Michigan. She appeared taken aback as we pulled up to the sandy beach. "Wait, you weren't joking, people really do surf in this area?" she said incredulously.

"Absolutely," I responded.

"Would you be up for giving it a shot tomorrow?" I inquired.

"Absolutely!" Ava responded with enthusiasm, "You won't need to ask me twice!"

The next morning, I rose early, gathering my longboards and wetsuits, I stowed them in my car before heading out to pick up Ava. Arriving at the lake side, the water was calm and glassy. After donning our wetsuits, we paddled out and waited for the perfect wave. When it arrived, Ava sprung to life, popping up on her board, she rode it all the way to shore, laughing joyfully. I knew then that bringing her to this special place was the right thing.

Over the next few weeks, the bond between Ava and I grew stronger. We worked on a history project together about Ancient Mesopotamia, which involved more goofing off than actual work. She came over to my house one weekend and we made cookies and binge-watched Stranger Things with a big bowl of popcorn between us.

Bit by bit, Ava started to lower her guard with me. As the weeks went on, she began confiding in me more and more. Where at first she was closed off and reticent, she slowly became more forthcoming and openhearted. By taking things slowly and allowing her to warm up in her own time, I was able to gain Ava's trust.

She told me how hard it had been to leave her friends in San Diego, and that her relationship with her dad was pretty strained ever since her parents got divorced last year. I talked to her about my own family drama with my older sister being away at college and my mom getting laid off from her job. It felt good to have someone to confide in.

Before I knew it, October arrived, and we headed out to the Great Lakes for our last surfing experience before the season ended. We woke up early Saturday morning to catch the waves at their best. The sky was steely grey and the fall air crisp, a far cry from San Diego's eternal sunshiny warmth.

"So, what do you think so far of surfing on the Great Lakes?" I asked Ava eagerly as I finished waxing my board.

She took a deep breath before answering, "It smells so fresh and woodsy." Observing the lush green environment, Ava dipped her toe into the water and with a slight shiver, added, "The water is so cold."

I chuckled and tossed her one of my thickest wetsuits. "Here, this should help. Trust me, once you catch your first wave, you won't even notice the temperature."

We donned our gear and ventured into the slate-blue water. Perched on our boards, we awaited the perfect swell. Within minutes, I caught sight of a promising wave forming on the horizon.

"This one is a winner."

"Sporti, are you ready?"

Sporting a grin from ear to ear, Ava screamed out, "Let's do this," as she energetically and swiftly paddled out to align herself.

We both turned and began stroking hard across the building wave. I glanced over and saw Ava spring up flawlessly just as the swell barrelled around her.

"Woo hoo," she cheered, with a wild look of exhilaration as she sliced fluidly under the curl and for a moment, I lost sight of her behind the glistening tube. Suddenly she shot out the other side, whooping excitedly with her arms raised triumphantly overhead.

"Yeah, Ava, you go girl," I shouted after her. Man, that girl could surf! We continued to surf the waves of Michigan for more than an hour, which left us with freezing hands and aching muscles from all the exertion.

Finally, frozen and exhausted, we dragged ourselves and our boards back onto the beach before collapsing onto our towels.

"Not bad for your first fall experience surfing on the Great Lakes!" I grinned over at her. A few escaped blonde strands of hair clung to Ava's face and her cheeks were rosy from the biting wind.

"That was amazing," she beamed. "The waves here are different to those in Cali, but I love the quiet and peacefulness in Michigan. No competitive crowds trying to fight for a spot."

"So you approve of our junky little waves then?"

She giggled and playfully flung her towel at me. "Junky! I'd say those waves were totally epic!"

We lay there, chatting and joking around, while our wetsuits dried, savouring every ray of sun that kissed our faces. What began as a typical Saturday transformed into a remarkable autumn day.

Eventually, Ava sat up with a content little sigh. "As awesome as this has been, I should probably get home. I promised my dad I'd make dinner tonight." She stood and began unzipping her tight black wetsuit, peeling the neoprene off inch by inch until just her mint green bikini remained.

I made a concerted effort to refrain from staring, yet I found it challenging to divert my gaze from such an utterly captivating sight. Ava wrung the great lake water out of her long blonde waves, before slipping into a pair of alluring shorts and a cozy hoodie. I cleared my suddenly dry throat and looked away, busying myself with packing up my gear.

We tossed our boards into the bed of my pickup and I drove Ava back to her house. As we pulled up to the curb, Ava turned to me somewhat hesitantly.

"Would you consider joining me for dinner this evening?" she inquired with a hopeful tone. "I can't promise that the culinary experience will be exceptional, but I would appreciate your company."

My heart did a little leap. "I'd never say no to free food," I joked. She grinned and together we headed inside.

Ava showed me to the bathroom where I could freshen up, before making her way into the kitchen. Soon the tantalising scent of roasted vegetables wafted throughout the house. Wait, what is that heavenly smell ... is that maple bacon that I'm smelling? Now, I was seriously impressed with her hidden skills. Entering the kitchen, I rounded the corner to see an impressive curly-haired pig snuffling around the kitchen floor, searching for scraps.

Ava laughed and scooped up the wriggling pink bundle. "And this little troublemaker is Bacon Bits! Careful, he might nibble on your toes if you're not paying attention."

I scratched behind Bacon Bit's floppy ears as he oinked happily. "Nice to meet you Bacon Bits."

I hung out with Ava in the cosy farmhouse-style kitchen, while she sautéed veggies and fried eggs. Ava even allowed me to help out with the flipping of the pancakes. Revealing my lack of culinary skills when I burned the first one. Oops! At long last, the cooking session drew to a close, and we eagerly loaded our plates with steaming food before gathering around the cosy, rustic wooden table positioned by the window.

Wow Ava, this tastes amazing! You have so many hidden talents, I never realised that you could cook so well!" I told her before indulging in a substantial and delectable mouthful of veggie hash.

"Why do you sound so surprised?" Ava asked in mock offence, flicking a carrot at me across the table. "I may be a California girl, but I have more hidden skills than just surfing!" We both laughed.

Just then, the front door opened and Ava's dad walked in, dressed in his utility company uniform.

"Something smells good in here! Whatcha guys making?" he asked jovially, hanging up his keys and hat.

"Hi, Dad, this is my friend Andi from school," she introduced me.

"Nice to meet you, sir," I said politely, standing up to shake his hand.

"Likewise! And please call me Phil," he smiled warmly. "Glad to see Ava's already making friends around here."

Ava quickly fixed a plate for her dad. Soon the three of us were chatting over dinner, getting to know each other. Phil told me about their cross-country road trip from San Diego to Michigan, which sounded like they had filled it with plenty of wild adventures. And when I talked about local spots I liked to explore by the lake, he seemed genuinely intrigued.

Later that evening, as I grabbed my stuff to

head out, Ava walked me to the front door.

"Thanks for persuading me to go surfing today. And for everything... it's been kinda tough getting settled here, but you've made it feel more like home," she said softly, looking up at me through her lashes. I swallowed hard, hyperaware of how close we were standing in the dimly lit entryway.

"Being the new kid definitely rings a bell," I nervously confessed, sliding my hands into my pockets. "But you're a natural at making friends."

Ava's lips curved into a smile as she absentmindedly twirled her seashell necklace. Our gazes locked, and I found myself inexplicably drawn to her rosy lips. Was I interpreting these signals correctly? Before second-guessing myself, I leaned in gradually until our lips met in a tender kiss. A surge of excitement coursed through me as Ava embraced me, drawing me closer. We melded together seamlessly, like the missing piece of a puzzle falling into place.

After a few heart-pounding moments, I reluctantly pulled away, slightly breathless.

"Wow..." Ava whispered, her emerald eyes sparkling as she looked up at me.

"Yeah, um, wow, indeed," I stammered, still reeling from the moment.

"So, I'll see you at school on Monday?" she asked.

"Definitely!" I replied enthusiastically, flashing her a goofy grin. She returned one last dazzling smile before I floated towards my truck, feeling as light as air. But once inside, I couldn't resist releasing a rather unmanly victory squeal. Mateo would never let me live it down.

Ava and I were practically joined at the hip for the next couple of months. We studied together, went hiking and stargazing at state parks, and played video games at her place.

As Halloween drew nearer, I assisted her in creating homemade costumes for the occasion... she was a badass mermaid, and I dressed up as Aqua man. We won Mateo's neighbourhood costume contest together, which annoyed him to no end.

The holidays flew by in a blur of festive joy and too much eggnog. Before I knew it, Valentine's Day was approaching, and I still hadn't asked Ava to be my official girlfriend. I kept psyching myself out, worried it might mess up our easy dynamic.

"Dude, you gotta just make a move already! I swear if I have to watch you make heart eyes at blondie for one more week..." Mateo threatened at lunch one day.

"Dude, you're not getting it," I mumbled through a mouthful of pizza topped with pepperoni and cheese. "This girl is different. I've never had feelings this strong for someone before." I swallowed hard and took a swig of soda to force down the half-chewed pizza. "When I'm with her, it's like...everything else fades away. All I see is her. I know it sounds cheesy, but I think she might be the one." I took another bite from the doughy triangle in my hand, hoping the carbs would absorb the embarrassment flushing my cheeks. "What if she doesn't feel the same way?"

Mateo dismissed my concerns with an exaggerated eye roll. "Oh my God, grow a pair! That girl is clearly crazy about you. "Act quickly and make your move before another suitor sweeps her off her feet."

I knew Mateo was right. It was time to get over myself and just tell Ava how I felt. I came up with an awesome plan to take her on a sunset picnic overlooking the iced-over lake. There I would finally confess that I had fallen for her just as hard as she rode those waves.

On Valentine's evening, I picked Ava up, and we drove out to Bridgeman Bluffs as golden hour light bathed the snowy landscape. Luckily. the winding path down to the secluded beach was clear of ice. I spread out a cosy blanket and unpacked the feast of chocolate-covered strawberries, cheese, and other goodies I had prepared.

As the sun gradually descended in the sky, a hush fell over the forest. The vibrant melodies of birds gradually subsided, leaving a soft twitter in the air as they sought refuge for the night in their warm nests. Shadows stretched across the forest floor, enveloping the trees in dusk's embrace.

Ava and I sat at the now iced-up water's edge, watching the sky shift from blue to burnt orange. We munched happily, chatting about nothing in particular. I kept fiddling anxiously with the flower I had bought for her, trying to work up the courage. Pausing, I took in a deep breath, immersing myself in the crisp air infused with the aroma of pine needles.

"Remember how you thought it was funny I wore a wetsuit on that surf day in October? Well now, look at us... you totally fit in with us Michiganders!" I joked lamely, buying time.

Ava giggled and tossed a grape at me. "Maybe so! But I'll never give up my flip-flops and beach waves." Her golden hair practically glowed in the dimming light. She was so incredibly beautiful. It was now or never.

"Ava, I've been wanting to say something to you for a while now." With a gentle touch, I tucked the flower behind her ear, nestling it in her soft locks. The vibrant petals were a splash of colour against her golden waves, accentuating her features as the flower peaked out above her ear.

Gazing into her captivating eyes, I inhaled deeply, mustering the courage within me. "Ava..., from the moment we met, I felt a connection with you. A bond that I've never felt before. You make me happier than I ever thought was possible. Over these last few months, you've made me laugh harder than ever, try things I never would have imagined..."

I gently caressed her cheek with my hand. "You mean the world to me." I paused and smiled.

She tilted her head with an affectionate smile, waiting for me to continue.

I took another breath. "Well, I guess what I'm trying to say is... I'm completely falling for you."

Her dimpled grin grew impossibly wider. Before I even had time to worry about whether I'd made a mistake, Ava threw her arms around my neck, nearly knocking me backwards. "I've been falling for you too, you absolute dork! What took you so long?" she laughed against my collarbone, sending vibrations through my whole body.

I cupped her cold-flushed cheek with one

mitted hand. "So just to be clear... you'll be my Valentine then?"

"Well... let's see,... on one condition," Ava pretended to consider seriously.

"And what would that be?" I asked

 "That you'll be mine too!" She replied with joy in her voice.

"Well...I suppose I could do that," I chuckled. She responded by pulling me into a dizzying kiss that tasted like chocolate and happiness. Yep, Mateo owed me big time for actually working up the guts. But honestly? I was the real winner here.

Sophomore year flew past with Ava always at my side. We shared endless late-night conversations, embarked on adventurous day trips around Michigan on long weekends, and had cosy study sessions that often involved more cuddling than actual studying. But summer arrived too soon, bringing with it the inevitable separation.

Ava longed to return to California in July to visit old friends and family, and of course, to indulge in her passion for surfing. The bittersweet farewell day finally arrived, and I drove her to Metro Airport, holding her hand tightly all the way.

"I wish you didn't have to go," I whispered as

we unloaded her luggage outside the bustling terminal doors. Despite the chaos of the airport, Ava and I were in our own world, facing the dreaded goodbye we had been avoiding discussing for weeks.

I pulled her in closer, trying to imprint the feeling of her in my arms into my memory. "Skype me as soon as you land. Okay?" I said, my voice betraying my emotions.

She nodded, her green eyes moist with unshed tears. "I promise, and we'll video chat every day, just like always," she assured me.

Though she tried to reassure us both, her voice wavered, revealing her doubts. "I'll miss you like crazy," she admitted.

Swallowing hard, I whispered through her golden hair, "I'll miss you too. But junior year is just around the corner, full of adventures for us to embark on." Holding her close, the moment felt like a solemn commitment rather than just a passing dream.

The crackling boarding call for Ava's flight broke the moment. With a shaky exhale, she pulled me in for one last passionate kiss. I poured all my unspoken fears and promises into that goodbye kiss, hoping she could feel my unwavering devotion.

And then, she slipped from my embrace and disappeared down the terminal tunnel, stealing one last glance backward before vanishing from sight. I watched the plane ascend into the sky, carrying my heart thousands of miles away.

It saddened me to see her go, but I understood how much she missed the West Coast sunshine. We promised to stay in constant contact and plan a special reunion when she returned in late August.

The first week without my favourite blonde companion dragged on, leaving me feeling empty, since my sister was abroad on an art scholarship. Even attending a few neighbourhood parties with Mateo and dominating in pool volleyball couldn't shake off my gloomy mood.

Ava tried her best to keep me distracted during summer break by sending sweet selfies in front of iconic San Diego landmarks, and calling to gush about the awesome waves she'd ridden that day. It made me happy to see her having such a great time in her hometown. But hearing her stories still made me feel a little, disposable? Was Michigan just an extended stop for her, on her way to better things?

I kept those insecure thoughts to myself. The last thing I wanted was to ruin Ava's vacation or seem clingy. She deserved to fully enjoy this trip without feeling guilty for leaving her mopey girlfriend behind. I could handle a few weeks of moping if it made her happy.

After spending the best part of summer soaking up the California sun, it was time for Ava to return home to Michigan. It overjoyed me to know that she was returning, and I wasted no time picking her up at the airport. I had been looking forward to this day for weeks, eagerly counting down the days, then hours until I got to pick her up.

I excitedly headed out early towards the airport, anticipating the moment I'd see her walk through the gate. Impatiently, I paced around the arrival area, craning my neck, trying to spot her among the many passengers making their way out.

As I scanned the stream of passengers, I spotted her familiar smile lighting up the crowd. Excitedly, I waved, calling out her name. When our eyes met, it thrilled me to have Ava back after the long summer months apart.

Ava looked gorgeous with her bronze summer tan and sun-bleached hair. I hurriedly made my way towards her. Dropping her bags, Ava enveloped me in an intense bear hug. As our lips connected, the gentle texture of her rosy, full lips didn't go unnoticed.

On the drive home, we chatted about her West Coast adventures surfing the big tubes and soaking up the California sunshine. I told her about my uneventful summer spent working part-time at the ice cream parlour and binge-watching Netflix. It was comforting to fall back into the familiar patterns of conversation, and it felt like no time had passed at all.

CHAPTER THREE

Junior Year's Romance

AVA AND I were inseparable during the last weeks of summer, making the most of our time together before the demands of school took over. As summer faded into autumn and the first day of junior year arrived. Ava and I planned to meet in the car park before school.

After parking my car, I scanned the parking lot for Ava and spotted her across the way, gracefully seated on the hood of her car. As I strode toward her, the autumn leaves swirled around my feet, my pulse quickened with each step, and it felt as though my heart was about to burst from my chest. Upon reaching her, she slid sensuously off the hood, and we embraced tightly, sealing the moment with a tender kiss.

Gently gripping her waist, I took a step back, locking eyes with her captivating sea-green gaze. Inhaling deeply, and with unwavering confidence, I said, "We got this sporti, are you ready?"

We intertwined our arms and with heads held high we made our way towards the school, ready to confront the challenges of junior year head-on. As we crossed the threshold into the bustling high school hallway, a palpable sense of excitement enveloped us, hinting that this year was poised to be our most unforgettable yet.

History was our first class of the day, and our teacher, Mr Jensen, kicked things off with an intense group research project on the civil rights movement. Of course, Ava and I teamed up.

Each day after school, we would head to the library to work on our project. Picking through the dusty shelves, we gathered armloads of relevant books and started dividing up the research tasks.

Although the heavy workload kept us super busy through those first few weeks, it was nice having a mission to focus on together. We'd meet up after school and work for hours compiling notes, checking facts, and editing each other's drafts.

Upon completing the last tasks, we felt a mix of exhaustion and satisfaction, knowing we were ready. We finished our 25-page report and submitted it right on time, giving each other a good-natured high-five. Mr. Jensen's high level of satisfaction with the thoroughness of our project analysis earned us an A+ grade.

Like a beautifully written romance novel, our relationship continued to unfold in the most unexpected places. The academic challenges we faced together only strengthened the bond between us. Late-night study sessions and after-school activities transformed into moments of whispered confessions and stolen glances, rendering the intricacies of physics equations insignificant compared to the complexity of our feelings.

One evening, surrounded by the soft glow of study lamps and the scent of books, we found ourselves lost in the poetry of each other's presence. Our shared pursuit of knowledge became a dance, a symphony of intellect and emotion that echoed the beating of our hearts. In those quiet moments, our souls intertwined, creating a melody that resonated with the profound connection we shared.

Navigating the complexities of junior year wasn't just a journey through academics; it was an exploration of love in its purest form. Amidst the chaos of standardised tests and the looming uncertainty of college applications, Ava and I found comfort in the sanctuary of each other's arms. We became each other's refuge, a haven where the pressures of the outside world faded away, leaving only the warmth of our shared dreams.

Waking up, I noticed that the overnight snowfall had turned our small town into a frosted wonderland. The snow-capped trees and rooftops glistened with a layer of fresh powder. It was a magical start to the day. With the arrival of winter, Ava and I exchanged our surfboards for sledges. We made obligatory snowmen and raced our sledges downhill on the weekends until our cheeks stung from the cold and exhilaration.

The pristine blanket of snow meant the opening of the ice rink in town. Friday after school, we bundled up in thick jackets, opting to unwind with some frozen fun.

I stepped out on the ice first, arms extended gracefully to keep balanced. Ava clung to the wall, wobbling, trying to recall the basics of those skating lessons from so many years ago in California. The icy surface was a stark contrast to the Pacific waves that Ava was familiar with.

"C'mon slowcoach, you can do it!" I called back to her, effortlessly executing a flawless spin. "Show off," replied Ava

With caution, Ava pushed away from the wall, now wobbling more severely without support. Sensing her distress, I glided over and offered my mittened hands.

"Here, hold on and I'll guide you," I said gently. Gripping both her hands tightly, I began skating backwards, pulling her along the rink at a slow but steady pace.

After a few clumsy laps, Ava finally got her footing. I whooped proudly when Ava managed to skate a lap unassisted. We skated gleefully around the rink hand in hand until the Zamboni appeared, signalling closing time.

Plopping down on a bench to unlace our skates, I leaned over and bumped Ava's shoulder affectionately. "See, you're a natural! We make a pretty good team out there."

Ava chuckled. "Only cause I had the best teacher." But her faith in me did spark a brief rush of confidence. Together, we could take on any challenge.

Our affection flourished through the frosty winter months, strengthening and deepening like a hardy winter rose that blooms even in the coldest of conditions — thriving and lovely despite the icy weather surrounding it. We embraced the winter chill with mugs of hot chocolate topped with molten marshmallows and laughter-filled evenings of ice skating on the frozen lake, followed by intimate moments by the fireplace where our hearts danced to the crackling of burning embers.

Three weeks before Christmas break, Ava's father surprised her with box seat tickets he had won at work to see the San Diego Padres, which meant that they would fly back to California a couple of weeks before winter break.

For two weeks, a hollow ache filled my chest every time I passed the empty desk beside me in history class. I hadn't heard from Ava in a few days and I kept re-reading her last text from three days ago.

Saturday night, I was working on my AP calculus homework in my bedroom when I heard a familiar FaceTime ringtone. I quickly grabbed my phone, expecting to see Mateo's name pop up, ready to vent about the latest football drama. Instead, Ava's smiling profile pic and California area code flashed across the screen. Immediately, a surge of joy flooded through me, lifting my spirits too new heights.

"Ava! Hi!!" I answered enthusiastically. Just seeing her sun-kissed face felt like a breath of fresh ocean air filling my stale Michigan lungs.

"Andi! I'm sooo sorry I've been M.I.A lately. Things over here have been absolutely chaotic. All my Cali friends want to see me." She rolled her eyes dramatically. I'm only one person and cannot split myself into a hundred pieces. But I'm DONE making excuses! I can't stand us feeling so disconnected."

My chest warmed at her words. So I wasn't the only one feeling the distance take its toll.

"It's okay, I totally get it," I assured her. "We both just got swept away by life." We chuckled ruefully. Ava collapsed backwards onto a teal bedspread, groaning at the ceiling.

"Think positive. At least you get to enjoy that gorgeous ocean view to clear your mind instead of boring old cornfields," I pointed out. Suddenly her aunt's golden retriever, Sandy, bounded into view, attacking Ava's face with sloppy dog kisses.

"Ahh Sandy! Down girl!" Ava laughed, playfully shoving the hyper pup off her chest. I grinned, watching their silly antics, feeling that hollow place inside start to fill up again.

We ended up talking for almost two hours about everything under the sun. I told Ava all about Mateo's latest football drama and how my sister was apparently dating some pretentious artist guy in Prague. Meanwhile, she filled me in on the new vegan cafe she discovered by the beach. It felt amazing to just laugh and be totally unfiltered together like always... almost like no time or distance had passed at all.

I noticed Ava stifling a yawn behind her palm.

"Ah shoot, I forgot about the time difference! It must be super late there," I realised guiltily.

She waved off my concern. "It's fine. I'd stay up talking to you all night if I could.

I laughed sympathetically.

"Sooo winter break's coming up soon..." I started slowly. "What would you think about me maybe flying out there to visit for a few days?"

Ava's eyes instantly lit up. "Seriously?! You have no idea how much I'd love that."

I exhaled, relieved she seemed enthusiastic about the plan instead of weirded out.

"But how?" she asked

"My dad has a bunch of miles saved up from work trips that he said I could use. And I picked up some extra shifts at the movie theatre to help save cash too," I explained. This would be my first time travelling solo, but I was willing to navigate airports by myself if it meant seeing Ava again.

She clapped excitedly, making the video image shake. "Ahh, this is perfect! You'll get to experience a real San Diego Christmas—it feels nothing like snowy Michigan, I promise. Palm trees all decorated with twinkly lights, surfing in Santa hats..."

I laughed at her adorable animation, already imagining the halls decked out in seashells and flip-flops instead of holly wreaths. "Well, it definitely sounds memorable. Hopefully, Plane Ticket Santa comes through because I can't wait!"

On the first day of Christmas break, I found myself navigating the crowded terminals of San Diego International, my backpack stuffed with tee shirts and swim trunks completely unsuited for December. Mateo had driven me to Metro Airport at sunrise, blasting obnoxious breakup songs the whole way as "preparation for surviving long-distance life." What a great friend.

But his sarcasm was quickly forgotten when I stepped outside the arrivals lane into California's dazzling sunlight, scanning the busy pickup area for any sign of Ava. Commuters hugged their loved ones all around me, filling the morning air with happy exclamations. Still no glimpse of my favourite blonde though. I checked my phone again, wondering if I'd somehow missed instructions to meet elsewhere. Nope, she should be here any minute.

I found myself nervously scanning passing faces once more when suddenly a force crashed into me from behind, nearly knocking me off my feet.

"You're here!" a familiar voice squealed in my ear. Ava had leapt onto my back, wrapping her legs around my waist.

"Whoa there crazy!" I chuckled. All the tension instantly melted away at her touch. She smelled just like I remembered—coconut butter and fresh air and home.

Finally, Ava slid back down to the sidewalk, keeping her arms twined around my neck as I turned to face her. She looked even more radiant than I recalled, with sunny streaks threading through her windswept waves.

"Surprise cuddles are my forte," she said with a smug smile.

"But c'mon, let's get your stuff loaded. I

wanna take you straight to the beach, right now!"

Within minutes, we had piled into Ava's sky-blue Jeep Wrangler, cruising down the highway with the top folded back. Warm salty air whipped through my hair as I gawked at the palm trees and red-tiled roofs zooming past. I already understood why Ava missed this place so much. It felt so exhilarating just being here soaking up the sunshine, the colours and the ocean breeze.

We ended up spending the entire first day frolicking on Pacific Beach like two little kids—burying each other in the sand, and splashing in the turquoise water. At one point, we even built a lopsided sandcastle decorated with stranded kelp that Ava dubbed, "Chateau Sheldon."

I almost couldn't believe this was my life—laying on the white sand watching diamond waves crash, with a gorgeous, wild spirit of a girl curled up beside me. Everything about it seemed like a movie scene instead of reality. Part of me worried I'd blink and suddenly wake up back in my bedroom in snowy Michigan.

As the sinking sun lit the ocean ablaze in molten reds and oranges, Ava sat up and turned toward me, chewing her bottom lip nervously. Uh oh, that was never a good sign.

Before I could ask what was up, she blurted

out in a rush, "Okay, don't freak out, but... what would you say about making Cali more permanent?"

I bolted upright. "Wait, what? More permanent, how?" I tried reading her expression, but for once I couldn't decipher what she was thinking.

Ava fiddled with her seashell necklace, refusing to meet my gaze. "Well, it's just... you fit in so perfectly here, Andi. And I know you've always dreamed about moving somewhere warmer. So what if you stayed with me in Cali next semester and finished high school in San Diego?"

Whoa, definitely not what I expected. My mind spun, trying to absorb this idea.

"Permanently... I mean, I wish we could be together more than anything," I said carefully. "But why permanently, moving across the country is huge. What would even happen to my parents and everything back in Michigan?"

"My dad's contract will be finishing at the end of this semester and he is being transferred back to the San Diego office," Ava explained. "I have already spoken to him and he said he would call your parents when we get back to discuss details," Ava rushed on enthusiastically. "Come on, don't you want to ditch all that cold snow for an endless summer?"

I looked out at the fiery waves lapping the sand, an icy rock settling in my gut. As incredible as this place was, it somehow felt... off. Yeah, I complained about blizzards and dreary skies all the time back home. But I'd also built my entire life in Michigan, — friends, memories, a future I'd meticulously planned. Could I really just toss that all aside impulsively?

Seeing the pained look on Ava's face, I could tell this was about more than just physical distance. I took a deep breath and said gently, "Come here." I opened my arms and folded her into an embrace, her head nestling into the crook of my neck as if we were two halves of a whole. I held her close, hoping my arms could provide the comfort words couldn't. She melted against me, the tension in her muscles easing. Neither of us spoke as we swayed slightly, the silence saying more than language could capture. At this moment, the miles between us faded away.

"You know I also want us to be together more than anything. But San Diego's your home, not mine."

I sensed her exhale against my chest, a soft sigh that carried both contentment and apprehension.

"Being with you is incredible, but my life is in Michigan," I murmured gently, tracing circles on her back. "Long-distance is tough, but so is dropping everything for a spur-of-the-moment decision. It's not really a solution, you know?"

Ava nodded reluctantly, her expression tinged with sadness as I swept a stray strand of wind-blown hair from her face. "We still have the rest of winter break," I reminded her, tucking the golden strand behind her ear. "Let's make the most of the time we have together. Let's not dwell on goodbyes just yet."

Taking her hand in mine, I caressed her knuckles with my thumb. "I want to cherish every moment with you while we can. Let's create memories to hold onto."

She offered a melancholic smile. "You're right. But will you think about it? … For now, let's enjoy the present without worrying about the future."

Drawing her close, I inhaled the faint coconut scent of her shampoo. "Exactly, Winter break is ours," I affirmed, planting a kiss on her forehead. "Let's treasure every remaining moment together. The future can wait. How about we focus on making the most of it together?"

Finally, a small smile graced her lips as she hugged me tighter. "Deal. And I apologise for dropping this on you so suddenly. I just miss seeing your face in person, you know?"

"I understand completely," I reassured her,

glad to feel the tension easing. Holding her hands, I met her worried gaze. "I know it feels daunting right now. The distance, the uncertainty. But if there's one thing I'm certain of, it's this..."

Gently lifting her chin, I met her eyes. "You and I? We'll figure it out. No matter the obstacles, no matter the distance. What we share is special. It's the stuff of legends."

I grinned, squeezing her hands. "We'll find a way. I promise. Together, we'll craft our own story, Ava Wave. You and me, always."

She tilted her head to mine, her green eyes reflecting the warmth of the sunset. And in that moment, with the ocean's melody in the background, I knew I'd never doubt that promise again.

The rest of the break passed in a blur. Ava showed me her favourite spots, from hiking in Torrey Pines to indulging in tacos in Old Town, and even attempting to teach me how to surf (emphasis on attempting) in the ocean. Our evenings were filled with cheesy movies and Mario Kart tournaments with her friends, creating memories to last a lifetime.

Before I knew it, New Year's Eve arrived—my last night in paradise. Ava assured me that she was saving the best for last.

"Okay don't open your eyes yet!" she instructed later that evening, guiding me by the shoulders through what smelled like a heavily chlorinated room. I could hear voices and music already going somewhere nearby.

Finally, Ava stopped and let go. "Alright...now!"

I opened my eyes to find us standing at the edge of a huge crowded pool, orange string lights criss-crossing overhead. In the shallow fountain area, kids were breakdancing to thumping music. And splashing around the deep end, I recognised Ava's water polo teammates from photos.

"Surprise! Welcome to the biggest bash of the year," Ava declared, arms flung out proudly like a showgirl.

"Whoa, your friends throw parties in the school pool? That's freaking epic!" I said excitedly. Talk about ending the break with a splash.

The night passed in a blur of neon lights, dancing, and way more Marco Polo than any nearly-legal teens should logically play. Some of Ava's teammates even tried convincing us to sneak into the locked rooftop hot tub at midnight until she rolled her eyes and dragged me away. Mostly, though, we just laughed until our stomachs ached, savouring every last golden second together.

In the wee hours of 2022, we found ourselves sitting along the pool wall, her head leaning comfortably on my shoulder. By now the frenzied energy had calmed to a sleepy lull and only a few kids still splashed around.

I rubbed Ava's arm gently. "Is this how you West Coast kids bring in the New Year?" I teased, gesturing at the scene before us?

"Yep! Inappropriate and slightly illegal," she sighed contentedly. "Does this mean you'll come back next year?"

Her words carried a heavier weight though, hanging unspoken between us. We both knew winter break's magic only lasted so long. Soon I'd be flying away. A bittersweet twist clenched my chest when I thought too hard about leaving.

But Ava had brought me here to escape all that weight of reality—if just for one wild, starry moment in time.

I kissed her hair softly. "Couldn't imagine ringing it in anywhere else." And right then, I truly meant it.

Suddenly, everyone started loudly chanting the midnight countdown. "10...9...8..."

Ava straightened up to face me, eyes glimmering with reflected lights. "Here's to making some waves this year. Together, even if you're half a country away."

"5...4..."

I smiled, pulling her close. "I'll Skype you every day if I have to. No more disappearing acts."

"2...1...Happy New Year!" The pool suddenly resounded with enthusiastic cheers and playful splashes, creating an atmosphere filled with lively energy.

And as we kissed, fireworks flowered brilliantly outside, for those few timeless seconds distance and days ahead didn't matter. We had right now, and that shining glimpse of togetherness? Well, that was really all we needed to hold on to.

CHAPTER FOUR
New Year

THE HARSH BEEP of my alarm clock jolted me awake way too early the next morning. I fumbled blindly to silence it, visions of beach sunsets and neon pool lights still dancing behind my eyelids. But the fantasy quickly faded as I took in the pile of half-packed suitcases and the plane ticket on my bedside table.

Today marked the start of the New Year, and I was about to embark on the dreaded flight back home to snowy Michigan. Back to the real world and the business of junior year.

I dragged myself out of bed and got dressed on autopilot, triple checked I hadn't forgotten to pack anything. Soon we were loading bags into the back of Phil's car as I gazed down at Sandy's muddy paw prints scattered across the driveway.

Ava's father drove us to the airport, with most of the journey passing in silence. Ava's hand clutched mine while Top 40 tunes hummed faintly on the radio.

With every passing mile, my stomach churned more intensely as the weight of reality settled in. In a couple of hours, I'd be staring out an aeroplane window, bidding farewell to this sunny paradise.

Ava and her father were set to follow in a couple of days. Those few days would seem interminable to me until I could reunite with my beloved sea-breezed blonde once more.

I could not have been hiding the storm clouds in my head as well as I thought because suddenly Phil pulled off the freeway into a beach overlook parking lot. He shifted the gear into park and turned off the engine. Turning to face us, he said, "We still have some time, and I believe you girls could benefit from a chat while I take a moment to stretch my legs."

Shifting closer, Ava gazed into my eyes. "Okay spill. What's going on in that brain of yours?" Her tone gave no room for pretending everything was fine. I sighed, picking at a fraying hole in my shorts.

"I...I just... really don't wanna leave this. Leave you." My voice cracked, embarrassingly. "What if being apart starts to ruin things?"

A mixture of emotions flashed across Ava's face—sadness, empathy, but also stubborn determination. She squeezed my hand, waiting until I met her fierce green gaze.

"Listen to me spill. It's only for a few days and anyway, we have already survived time apart at opposite ends of the country, right? And that was without even trying. It's not like it's forever, I'll be back in Michigan before you know it," she said with a reassuring tone.

I bobbed my head reluctantly. "I can't argue with facts."

"But for now?" Ava continued, "We know how to do this. How to stay close and make time for each other no matter how chaotic life gets. It's you and me, kelp for brains."

A small smile tugged my mouth at the old nickname. I really wanted to believe in her confidence that we could handle long distance again, despite my ever-present doubts.

Sea-salt scented air swirled through the open windows as Ava scooted closer, her words barely above a whisper. "Wanna know a secret?… I'm pretty terrified too."

My eyebrows shot up in surprise. Little Miss Sunshine afraid? But before I could respond, she rushed on.

"Moving back here at the end of junior year will feel like I'm leaving a piece of myself behind. And the thought of losing my lover, my best friend, the person who made Michigan feel like home for me." Her voice caught.

"It's my worst nightmare. Like maybe everyone who matters will always just... leave."

Seeing Ava so openly vulnerable clenched my chest. Without hesitation, I wrapped her in a fierce hug, hoping my embrace could somehow mend the gaps wedged between us.

"You'll always have me—you dork, you know

that, right?" I murmured into her hair.

Ava nodded against my shoulder, sniffling slightly. "I'm just really dreading walking out those airport doors alone. But we'll be okay, right?"

"Always," I promised again. And I meant it with every last aching fibre of my being.

We sat like that for a few moments longer, drawing strength from each other's touch. Finally, Ava pulled back with the faintest hint of a smirk.

"I know California's secretly your soulmate," she teased with a dramatic eye flutter. "And I know you going to miss the beach and those delicious burgers"

I let out an unexpected chuckle, giving her a playful nudge on the shoulder. "Ah, I see how it is now. I'm just your beach buddy and an In-N-Out burger companion, huh?"

"Duh! Why, what else did you think?" Her giggles gradually softened into a genuine smile as she reached over, grazing my jaw tenderly with her thumb. "Nah, its mostly cause I'm pretty crazy about you."

A comforting sensation enveloped my chest, despite the lingering ache. No matter how many states separated us, I could endure the distance, knowing I still held Ava's heart. We sealed that unspoken promise with a slow, lingering kiss—a lifeline to cling to in the coming lonely days.

Before we knew it, we were standing outside departures, while the parking attendant helped to unload my bags.

After loading my luggage onto the trolley, we made our way indoors for a final cup of coffee, as Ava's dad leisurely browsed through the magazines available for sale. Sitting across from Ava, I found myself drawn into the depths of her mesmerising green eyes. With her hands tightly clasped in mine, I made a conscious effort to etch every intricate detail of her presence into my memory, like capturing a mental snapshot to cherish forever. The early sunlight filtering through the window highlighted Ava's golden waves of hair. Her tear-filled eyes glimmered against the cloudless blue sky behind her. A hint of chocolate smeared across her left cheek, remnants of the doughnut we enjoyed together.

"Less than a week," Ava said with forced lightness. But I caught the wistful glint behind her smile.

In an instant, a haze clouded my vision, tears pooling at the corners of my eyes, ready to cascade down my cheeks. With a deep breath, I stood up, gently dabbing at my eyes, as I made my way closer to Ava, and settled down beside her.

Before I could get all emotional, Ava grabbed my shoulders, her expression abruptly shifting to hyper-seriousness.

"Okay listen, I know long distance sucks majorly," she stated, her green gaze boring intensely into mine. "But it clearly can't break us apart, since we're both still sitting here. You are about to get on that plane and head back to snowy Michigan, right?"

I blinked, surprised by her abrupt shift in tone.

A little softer she added, "So just remember that whenever you start overthinking things. Not even 3,000 miles can ruin this bond."

I huffed a tearful half-laugh. Only Ava could deliver the most punch-to-the-gut, poetic wisdom while also looking completely adorable.

And somehow it was exactly what I needed to hear.

"You're kinda the best ever. You know that?" I told her sincerely, my heart swelling two sizes. Before she could respond, I swept her up into one last spine-popping hug, wishing I could just stuff this amazing human into my carry-on bag right now.

Before I knew it, the boarding call for my flight crackled over the PA system. With a resigned sigh, Ava slowly unwound herself from my clinging koala grip and we made our way over to the departure gate.

"Well…This is it. Farewell for real this time. Call me when you land… okay?" Her brave facade now visibly crumbled at the edges. "And you better not forget about me back there in snow-land."

"Never possible." I squeezed her hand, etching the feeling of her palm against mine into memory. "Stay golden, Ava Wave."

And with a final kiss, I forced my jelly legs to walk through the automatic doors alone.

True to her word, Ava kept us tethered close despite the distance. We texted constantly—sometimes deep reflections about the future and other times goofy observations that made zero sense out of context. We even streamed movies together until one of us inevitably fell asleep mid-scene.

The constant check-ins made the long days feel less gaping and lonesome. And even when life drowned us separately in its chaos, simply hearing Ava's voice anchored me home again. This whole long-distance thing was admittedly very messy, but together we were making it work.

I missed Ava's bubbly energy and adventurous spirit. Things just seemed duller and greyer without my favourite blonde around. But soon she would be on her way back, and the anticipation made it feel like the sun was about to come out again.

I headed to the airport early in the morning on the day she was due to arrive. Pacing around arrivals, I craned my neck, trying to spot her. Then, from out of nowhere, I heard quick footsteps, followed by a blur of blonde hair crashing into me.

"Andi!" Ava squealed, nearly knocking me over with the force of her hug. I squeezed her back tightly, once again feeling whole, knowing that I had my other half beside me.

On the drive home, Ava chatted endlessly and happily about her last few California adventures as white flakes swirled and danced outside the foggy windows. I smiled contentedly, one hand on the wheel while the other held hers tight, our fingers interlaced.

The next morning, life returned to normal, and we were back in the halls at school, starting our second semester of junior year. And just like that, Ava seamlessly slipped back into Michigan's life. We aced our history test on the Cold War and she made me laugh until I cried at lunch, recounting funny stories about her childhood in California.

At times, I caught her gazing wistfully at the grey, icy landscape outside. I knew a part of

Ava's heart would always remain tied to sunny California. But then she'd turn back with a soft smile that assured me that Michigan now felt just as much like home with me by her side.

On Valentine's Day, I surprised Ava with a bunch of red roses and a playlist I'd titled "Reasons I Love You" filled with all cheesy romantic songs. In return, she gave me an adorable care package stuffed with classic beach essentials: lemon soap that smelled just like her, peppermint lip balm, and a shiny new snorkel and mask. At the very bottom, I found a starfish keychain with a note that said:

A tiny piece of me to have wherever you roam this year. We got this! Xoxo — Ava

I clipped it proudly to my backpack zipper, so I would glimpse at the glittering green plastic every time I grabbed for my chem notes. Just a trinket, sure, but it carried the weight of Ava's steadfast heart.

The winter weeks flew by, filled with pep rallies, snowball fights, and spontaneous dance parties in my kitchen. Ava never failed to make everyday moments fun and special. With her here, the future seemed bright with hope and promise no matter what uncertainties senior year held.

So while I knew our junior year days were nearing the inevitable end, I chose to cherish each glowing moment spent with Ava. Time together now was a gift to carry fondly in our hearts.

And through it all, one unshakable truth remained—the summer girl with sea-glass eyes had permanently changed my little corner of the world for the better. Her effervescent energy is a constant beacon, illuminating the darkest of nights like a radiant star guiding my way.

With summer camp job interviews, AP tests looming, and the pressure of college decisions brewing, most days I had very little free time for myself. In California, Ava's water polo squad accomplished something truly remarkable by qualifying for regionals. Meaning that they eagerly expected her return for the summer.

Even with our hectic schedules, Ava and I never went longer than a day or two without at least an emoji-filled text. But with Ava's imminent return to California, our conversations lacked their usual colour. Fleeting five-minute phone calls couldn't capture the full spectrum of our messy inner worlds anymore. Staring at Ava's tiny pixelated face during video chats, I tried to reconcile this ghost version with the sun-drenched girl who still dazzled clearly in my memory.

The thought of Ava leaving Michigan at the

end of the semester weighed heavily on me. When you're a 17-year-old, everyone wants to map out your entire future for you in concrete. But all I craved was adventuring through the fleeting now with my favourite human by my side.

Curled on my bedspread staring numbly at algebra equations one dreary Wednesday evening, my phone suddenly lit up with Ava's ringtone. I grabbed it on the second vibration.

"Ava! Hi!" I answered too quickly, like a desperate puppy. Smooth, dude. Real smooth, get a grip!

But she either didn't notice the over-eager edge to my voice or simply chose not to poke fun at it this time.

"Hey you! Feeling spontaneous at all?" Ava asked. Was that... nervous energy swirling underneath her breezy tone, too?

I sat up, intrigued. "I mean spontaneous is your love language. So I'm guessing this isn't just a social call?"

"Wow, nothing gets past you, Sherlock! But for real, what are you doing during spring break?" Something definitely seemed up. I could practically hear the excited sparks crackling through the phone.

My interest doubled, but I tried playing it cool.

"I think I had some exhilarating extra calculus scheduled, but it's probably fine to postpone it for something more enjoyable. Why, do you have something in mind?"

"Perfect! Then pack your bags, babe. We're going to California!"

I froze, my heart rocketing into my throat. Surely I must've misheard her.

"Wait... did you just say California as in flying across the entire country again?" I stammered.

Ava's laughter bubbled through the speaker. "Well, it's not the one in Canada! C'mon, you know I'm last minute. I hope that's alright?" Her voice turned uncertain and fragile, with a hope I didn't dare crush.

"Alright? Ava, it's freaking fantastic!" I whooped, punching the air victoriously. A spontaneous trip to sunny paradise with my favourite girl? Obviously, I wasn't gonna say no!

We stayed up late into the night, finalising plans, gushing about all the memories we'd make during this surprise trip. For the first time in weeks, talking to Ava recaptured that easy magic—the kind of conversation that flows unfiltered and wild like it could never run dry.

I fell asleep imagining the California sunshine soaking into my skin once more. Yet, even more delightful than the prospect of sandy beaches was the anticipation of the precious moments I would share with Ava.

CHAPTER FIVE

Spring Break

A WEEK LATER at baggage claim, I was bouncing on my heels, scanning the bustling crowd with my gorgeous blonde by my side. An elderly couple we'd sat next to on the plane waved politely as they passed by with their luggage. Moments later, Ava's luggage appeared on the carousel and shortly afterwards, mine. Grabbing our bags, we headed towards the exit and into the bright California sunlight to find a taxi.

Wrapping my arms around Ava, I pulled her in closer. Ava tilted her face up, nose crinkling adorably. "What're you smiling all goofy for?"

"I'm just... really freaking happy to be here with you," I admitted, warmth flooding my chest.

"Well, the feeling's beyond mutual," Ava sighed against my shoulder. Neither of us made any move to break apart just yet. "Thank you for surprising me like this." I whispered through her golden strands.

The sun-drenched days that followed, passed in a blur of saltwater and laughter. We plunged into our own little world—just the two of us suspended in time as we soaked up every second with each other.

Most mornings we'd grab acai bowls topped with pineapple and wander towards the tidal pools hand-in-hand. Intently scouring for vibrant anemones. Sometimes we were fortunate enough to spot dolphins arcing effortlessly through the aqua waves, their sleek grey forms glinting like liquid mercury. I'd never seen Ava's eyes flash so brilliantly.

By early afternoon, when the fog had evaporated into the sweltering golden heat, we'd sprawl shirtless on the blistering sand, pitting avocados with chips and lime. A ridiculous debate once sparked over whether seagulls make better pets than pigeons. Another day I smeared zinc across Ava's cheeks in a very accurate walrus impersonation.

Eventually, we'd drag our sun drenched bodies out into the refreshing shallows of the Pacific Ocean until our fingertips pruned. Inevitably this would lead to splash fights erupting as I tossed Ava over my shoulder in an effort to dunk her underwater.

Her shrieks of indignation always morphed into breathless laughter, and that dimpled smile glowed brighter than the setting sun? Her contagious laughter, filled me with honey-golden warmth from head to sandy toe.

I couldn't remember the last time someone's company charged the air between us with such rollicking joy. Every colour here somehow seemed to be amplified, like Ava herself. She radiated with dazzling technicolour energy.

By Friday, we had not discussed the topic of our imminent departure on Sunday. We both wordlessly understood that once acknowledged, reality would come crashing down. So, I pushed the worries about our inevitable return to Michigan's monochrome landscape from my mind. That night we camped out on the beach, watching meteors streak across spring's inky sky.

Tomorrow could wait; for now, I craved more stardust-silver moments with Ava, tracing constellations.

The shrilling blast of a train whistle jolted me from my dreams early the next morning. I jolted upright, momentarily disoriented by sunlight dappling through swaying palms instead of my usual curtains.

Ava mumbled incoherently, sand crusted across her left cheek. As my vision adjusted, I spotted a messy blonde bedhead lying beside me. Reality clicked back into focus.

Tomorrow was departure day. In a few short hours, we'd be exchanging this oceanic dreamscape for Michigan's monotone grey landscape once again. The mere thought sent my mood sinking faster than the receding tide.

I really didn't wanna disturb Ava yet, but I knew time was an unsympathetic mistress. We reluctantly untangled from our cosy sand nest, shaking out crumbs and broken seashell shards.

The drive back to her house remained unusually quiet, except for the Top 40 tunes humming faintly on the radio. I could practically hear worries beginning to bubble in Ava's thoughts, about surviving more months in snowy Michigan. Honestly, I was trying not to spiral down that black hole myself.

I kept sneaking glances over at her, hardly believing this sun-kissed beach goddess beside me was the same girl I'd fallen for in sophomore year. Back when she seemed so shy and guarded. Now Ava brimmed with glowing confidence—as effervescent as the foamy breakers she conquered effortlessly.

Her golden hair streamed out the open Wrangler windows as we sped along the coastal highway. The early California sunlight ignited those natural honey highlights, evoking memories of joyous laughter amidst sunset hues painted across the water earlier this week. Like Ava herself, this electrifying paradise burrowed beneath my skin as if it had always belonged there.

I shook away the traitorous thoughts before nostalgia's riptide could pull me under. No use getting attached when in a few hours we'd once again be jetting through the clouds away from paradise... beside me, the girl who embodied summer's dazzling spirit.

As we pulled up outside Ava's little rancher

accommodation, I choked down the bitter aftertaste of goodbye threatening to crush my lungs. I should savour this glowing morning in paradise with her instead of moping prematurely.

A refreshing ocean breeze tumbled lazily down the sun-baked street as I unloaded bags from the Wrangler's trunk. Meanwhile, Ava pried off her flip-flops by the front door, revealing a fresh coat of metallic turquoise polish on her toes. I smiled to myself, remembering how I painted them just a few nights ago as we shared a bottle of smuggled rosé on her back patio.

Manicures under the stars had become our unofficial tradition, ever since sophomore year when Ava attempted to do my nails drunk on boxed wine at 2 AM. Let's just say the results were a disastrously smudged mess, that took over three rounds of remover before my cuticles stopped resembling a unicorn slaughter scene. Among the multitude of snapshots, there lurked an embarrassing photograph, immortalising Mateo in fits of hysterical laughter at my misfortune.

There was a certain comfort in the gentle touch of Mateo as he skilfully applied the creams and colours to my hands, his demeanour free of any judgment towards my amateur salon techniques. Other dudes might mock something so intimate or feminine. Secretly, Mateo found the creative process weirdly soothing even when completely sober... this was a stark contrast to his initial attempt at something sparkly, which was far from tranquil.

I'd noticed when saying goodbye on New Year's, Ava wore that same metallic turquoise polish in tribute. At the time, I figured it was just coincidence or convenience. Looking at her adorable toes now, I pondered whether she deliberately selected it as a nostalgic reference to happy memories.

"Earth to Andi?" Ava's teasing voice suddenly cut through my nostalgic mental meanderings. "Are you planning on helping to carry stuff inside, or are you just going to stand there staring and grinning at my feet?"

I felt an embarrassed flush creeping up my neck as I hastily grabbed the rest of the bags and followed her through the front door. So much for subtle smoothness.

We dumped our sandy clothes in the garage hamper, then Ava disappeared to shower while I started a load. I could hear her belting Katy Perry from the bathroom as I surveyed leftovers in the fridge for brunch.

Twenty minutes later Ava strolled into the kitchen wearing ripped cut-off shorts and a loose Billabong shirt. Her citrus shampoo scent mingled temptingly with the frying onions and sizzling eggs. Damn, she looked unfairly cute with messy wet hair and owlish red glasses slipping down her nose. I slyly tried fixing my disastrous bedhead before she noticed.

"Soooo what's the chef got cookin'?" Ava asked, popping a stray chunk of avocado in her mouth.

"Your wish is my command, m'lady. We've got a gourmet scramble with eggs, cheese, avocado, onion and turkey bacon coming right up!" I swept my arm out with an exaggerated bow. Laugh crinkles etched around her eyes.

"Well, as long as that bacon's extra crispy, you know I'm sold!"

We dug into the tasty scrambled medley picnic-style out on the back patio, yellow sunlight filtering through swaying palms. A perfect ocean breeze kept the worst heat at bay. Seagulls wheeled raucously overhead, eyeing our platter with envious beady eyes. But for once, the present moment stretched untethered ahead of us with no painful imminent departure looming.

At one point, Ava tried tossing bits of egg toward two squirrels chasing each other around the lawn chairs. They scampered wildly, trying to catch every stray missile, their chittering almost sounding like laughter. Soon we both dissolved into breathless giggles, watching the Bushy Tail army's comedic acrobatic feats.

As the laughter finally subsided, Ava turned to me with a contented little sigh. "Mmm I'm really gonna miss this. Being here with you, just feels so easy and fun, you know?"

I scrubbed a hand through my tangled hair, hoping she didn't notice the blush creeping up my neck. "Oh trust me, I get it. This makes the idea of being buried under snowdrifts again, seem like actual torture."

"Hey, no talk of blizzards allowed in sunny California!" Ava chided, flicking my knee playfully. I feigned an indignant yelp.

"But honestly," she said more gently, "you just have this way of making everything... brighter and more colourful, if that doesn't sound super cheesy."

"Kinda does honestly. But cheesy in the best way," I teased lightly. Inside, though, every word spread golden flutters through my chest. Making someone's whole world shine brighter sounded like an impossibly huge legacy.

Ava absently brushed sandwich crumbs off her lap, her lower lip caught between her teeth. "Do you think that's dumb? I mean, we're not even living together for real but..."

"Hey, of course not," I cut in gently. Waiting until uncertain green eyes met mine again, I took her hand, tracing the purple polish still perfectly intact.

"I hope you know being here with you feels like the most vibrant, sun-drenched dream. And leaving this paradise sucks so hard every single time." I hesitated slightly. "But we'll make it to the end of the semester, and when you move back, I'm not gonna lose you just because of distance."

Some of the tension visibly melted from Ava's frame as her fingers tightened almost desperately around mine. And in that heartbeat, I wanted nothing more than to pull her close, promising we'd conquer space and time and every impossible odd. That somehow we would emerge still orbiting the other's side.

I tamped down the nearly overwhelming urge to suggest something crazy and irresponsible—like me moving here more permanently—knowing that definitely wasn't the solution either. At 17, with college on the horizon, our lives were full of unwritten possibilities.

But right then, none of that mattered. In this suspended moment, as rays of sunshine wound through the swaying palms, the sunlight highlighted Ava's honey hair. Tomorrow could worry about itself.

I let my thumb trace slow circles along her wrist until I felt the last nervous energy unwind from Ava's body.

"Well, when I move back, I don't plan on

losing you either, miss," she finally murmured. "Even when you're buried four feet under snow, I'll be bugging you hourly. Fair warning, pumpkin."

A wisp of a smile lifted my cheeks. "I would expect absolutely nothing less."

We slipped into easy conversation after that, skirting away from farewell's lingering storm cloud for now. Laughter and ridiculous debates flowed unhindered once more—our language of comfort.

Ava distractedly shuffled a deck of cards, trying to teach me some complicated game called Egyptian Rat Screw. I mostly just slapped at the pile chaotically, much to her endless amusement.

"No, you have to pay attention to sandwiches! That's literally the easiest rule," she insisted through giggles after having to explain the proper slap technique for the millionth time.

I threw my cards down in dramatic defeat. "Ugh, I suck at this! Can't we do something simpler like Go Fish?"

"Absolutely not; That's way too boring. C'mon, focus up!" Ava squared her shoulders, expression shifting to mock seriousness. "This is war, soldier!"

For the next hour, she ran me through drill session after drill session, on appropriate card slap reflexes and what exactly qualified as a sandwich. I'm pretty sure my failure to pick up strategies frustrated Ava's competitive spirit. But the adorable little crease between her brows whenever I messed up a painfully obvious play was worth it.

Eventually, she forfeited our practice match, gathering up the cards with an amused sigh. I couldn't resist reaching over to smooth the wrinkle still visible between her eyebrows before she swatted my hand away playfully.

"You're impossible, you know that?" But tender amusement lurked beneath Ava's faux exasperation. She leaned into me slightly as we watched the fading sunset paint the western sky into peachy water-coloured hues.

I mindlessly toyed with the loose strands of her hair, savouring the memory of those gold-like silk strands between my fingers.

"Impossibly charming, you mean?" I joked after a moment, hoping to steer us away from melancholy.

Ava rolled her eyes dramatically. "Uh no, just regular impossible." But her dimple betrayed a hint of a smirk.

I gasped loudly, clutching my heart. "You wound me! And to think I almost beat your winning Rat Screw streak back there."

"Yeah, if by 'almost' you mean not even

close." Ava dissolved into giggles again, face scrunching adorably. "Face it—I totally dominated your sad card-slapping skills."

"Keep talking smack and I'll throw you in the ocean, Wave Girl," I threatened with mock seriousness, wiggling my fingers toward her ribs. She recoiled instantly from the tickle attack, nearly tumbling off the lounge chair before I caught her waist to stabilise the clumsy flailing.

"Not if you can't catch me first!" Ava taunted. And as quick as a seagull she leapt up, vaulting easily over the half wall before sprinting barefoot across the sandy yard towards the beach.

I scrambled after her, the wind roaring in my ears mingled with sparkling laughter. "Oh, it is so on now! You just activated my Tackle Monster!"

But despite my longer legs, Ava kept agilely evading every lunge while trash-talking over her shoulder. We probably looked absolutely insane wrestling towards the surf as a fiery sunset stained the horizon with dreamlike watercolours.

Finally, I managed to snake an arm around Ava's waist mere feet from the lapping tide, spinning us both sideways into sugar sand. We crashed down, giggling breathlessly, my face hovering just above Ava's. Her eyes scrunched from laughing so hard, bits of gold hair clinging wildly across her damp cheeks. I pinned her flailing limbs beneath me, caging her body so she couldn't continue escaping.

"Caught ya," I panted triumphantly.

"Okay fine, you got me Tackle Monster," Ava conceded with one last hiccupping chuckle. She relaxed back into the sand, grin softening as her thumbs idly traced the lines of my forearms bracketed around her.

Gentle swells lapped a murmured rhythm a few feet behind us, filling the intimate bubble wrapped just around our connected forms. Dusk seeped violet and indigo through the darkening sky, faint first stars winking alight overhead.

Time appeared to stand still as I gazed down at Ava, glowing ethereally in my arms. It felt like we were in our own private, tilted reality, where an endless loop of blissful moments stretched out before us instead of this temporary farewell from paradise.

Some magnetic force drew me incrementally closer until barely a breath separated us. Ava's eyes dropped briefly to my mouth, then lifted again, sea glass irises pulling me like the tide toward her. Warm fingertips grazed my jaw tentatively... an unspoken question hovering there.

Before I could second guess, I dipped my head, letting my lips capture hers. She took a soft breath, instantly returning my kiss with a hunger and eagerness that reminded us of gasping for our first breath of air.

A dizzying sensation sparked everywhere we connected, blocking out anything beyond this small patch of sand cocooning us in our own whirling universe. My fingers threaded through Ava's wind-tossed waves, angling us impossibly closer until no atom of space remained. We kissed passionately and slowly under the muted purpling sky, stealing the very breath from each other's lungs as if we could halt time itself. And for that single flawless instant together, nothing else mattered but the taste of her mouth on mine.

As our lips met in a tender dance, the world around us seemed to fade away into a hazy background, leaving only the two of us enveloped in the soft glow of the purpling sky. In that single, flawless instant, the only thing that mattered was the flavour of her tender lips pressed against mine. The surrounding air carried a gentle breeze, teasing our hair and caressing our faces, creating an intimate atmosphere that matched the intensity of our connection.

The muted hues of the sky above mirrored the quiet passion between us, casting a dreamlike ambiance upon the scene. The sun, having dipped below the horizon, left behind soft shades of purple that blended seamlessly, creating an otherworldly palette. It was as if the universe itself conspired to set the stage for this moment of mutual longing.

The connection of our interlaced lips seemed to merge our very essence into one, as if our souls were uniting in a profound embrace. A kiss that transcended the physical and connected us on a profound and spiritual level. For a blissful moment, nothing else existed but the two of us, as we explored the depths of each other's emotions through the language of our intertwined mouths. Each stolen breath felt like a shared secret, a silent agreement that this moment was sacred and untouchable.

The rest of the world faded away as we lost ourselves in each other, our essences merging into one. It was a kiss that touched our innermost beings, affirming a bond that went far beyond the physical. Our hearts, minds, and souls came together in that kiss, uniting us in a way neither of us had experienced before. Although a brief moment in time, it was a kiss we would never forget, for it connected us on the deepest level two people can share.

Amid that purpling twilight, the world melted away, leaving behind the raw authenticity of our connection. The taste of Ava's lips on mine was an elixir, a blend of emotions that ranged from sweet to sultry. It was a symphony of desire, a dance of vulnerability that bound us together in a tapestry of shared intimacy.

As we lingered in that flawless instant, the rest of the world ceased to exist. It was just the two of us, lost in the magic of our shared passion. In that singular moment, the weight of the world lifted, and nothing else mattered but the intoxicating sensation of being fully present with each other.

Bathed in the radiant glow of the evening sky, our kiss embodied the splendour of two hearts joining as one. With the canvas of the firmament as our backdrop, we revelled in love's sweet euphoria. Our spirits danced, captivated by the magic born when souls entwined. Under heavens awash in twilight's purple haze, we discovered enchantment in each other's arms. Our lips locked in a timeless moment, a hymn to the wonder of affection found there together, as day bowed to night.

In that fleeting moment of connection, our embrace became a living testament to the enduring power of beauty when kindred spirits intertwine. Our hearts synchronised in a silent symphony, and we found solace in the understanding that the colours of the sky may shift and change — from the vibrant blue of day to the tender hues of violet at dusk — but the essence of our connection remained steadfast. It was a whispered promise that, despite the inevitable transitions of time and circumstance, the beauty born from the convergence of kindred souls would persist, casting a timeless glow upon the canvas of our shared existence.

As the golden morning sun peaked through the curtains, the jarring blare of my phone alarm jarred me awake. I fumbled to shut off the offensive noise without untangling myself from Ava. Blearily, I registered the numbers 8:45 AM flashing across my locked screen.

Crap… flight back to Michigan left in less than 2 hours.

The wonderful dreamy floatiness clinging to my bones instantly evaporated. I squeezed my eyes shut with a pained groan, reality crashing back in full nauseating force.

"No no no, make it stop. This is illegal levels of early," Ava grumbled into my shoulder. I huffed a half-hearted chuckle against her hair, the sound brittle and hollow to my own ears.

We lay unmoving for a minute more, clinging desperately to the last diaphanous threads of peace wrapped within each other's arms. I knew once we unravelled this intimate tether anchoring us together; it was only relentless hours that remained before our return to Michigan and the real world.

I brushed my lips to her temple, wishing I could freeze time indefinitely. "As much as I wanna hide here with you all day, that flight won't wait, apparently."

Ava sighed heavily, her grip tightening almost painfully. "I hate leaving here so freaking much. You think our parents would notice if we just... never came home?"

"Doubtful." I smoothed back her rumpled hair, thumb tracing the crease between her brows until I felt Ava begin to relax. "But hey— we still have some time till summer, remember?"

She wrinkled her nose, clearly not placated. "That's still plenty of time together. I swear, as much as I hate the cold, not even a freaking blizzard will keep me away from you. I want this winter to last forever."

A surprised laugh burst from my chest—part amusement at her wishes, but also a raw ache echoing behind my ribs. If anyone could actually punt blizzards spitefully into oblivion through force of will alone, Ava possessed that fiery brand of determination.

Impulsively I framed her face in both my hands, gazing intently into uncertain sea glass eyes until the last worried tension unknotted from her body.

"Well, lucky for you, this winter lover's lips are sealed, as they are only for you," I joked lightly. But my solemn tone conveyed the deeper promise as I brushed a stray curl behind Ava's ear. "We'll be okay. A few more months of winter together, before summer carries you back here."

She studied me for a long, thoughtful moment before breaking into a tiny dimpled grin that warmed my soul.

"Okay, but before that happens, you have to let me draw a bikini sticker tan line on your back later. Then you can really pretend its beach season 24/7."

A surprised bark of laughter burst from my chest—part relief she seemed willing to rally, but also sheer amusement at the mental image. " You drive a hard bargain

CHAPTER SIX

Senior Year Applications

HAVING MADE THE difficult decision to move back to California with her dad at the end of the semester. The next significant step for Ava was to research out to schools where she could finish her senior year. As much as she loved her life in Michigan, a part of her secretly craved the familiarity of San Diego—the salty ocean air, colourful sunsets over the water, and weekends spent surfing with friends.

Ava browsed through listings for highly ranked public and private schools in San Diego, creating a spreadsheet to compare academic programs, extracurriculars, and campus culture. Her guidance counsellor sent over transcripts and recommendation letters for her to submit with each application.

While excited to potentially return to her hometown, anxiety also plagued her. What if she didn't get into any of her top choices and ended up somewhere totally unfamiliar? Or if the kids were cliquey, and she struggled to make friends? At least in Michigan, she had Andi and their close group of friends to face the senior year with.

Just thinking about saying goodbye to Andi twisted Ava's insides. They had dreamed for years about taking on these monumental "lasts" side by side—homecoming, college apps, graduation.

Ava stared mournfully, pacing around her

boxes piled up in the now bare bedroom, remnants of a life soon to be left behind. Part of her heart would always stay here in Michigan with Andi. But she also owed it to herself to spend senior year at home with her dad.

As Ava settled in front of her computer screen, the weight of her aspirations and fears pressed upon her shoulders. With a deep, shaky breath, she braced herself for the task ahead. The cursor blinked patiently in the empty text box, awaiting her response to the pivotal question: "Why do you want to attend Mission Bay High School?"

Hours of meticulous work had been poured into this final application over the weekend. Ava had meticulously crafted her answers, weaving her passion for the arts and swimming into each word. Mission Bay beckoned with its renowned creative writing program and prestigious swim team—it was the embodiment of her dreams.

However, amidst the allure of Mission Bay, lay the daunting reality of leaving behind everything familiar, including her steadfast companion, Andi. The mere thought of navigating a new environment without Andi by her side sent shivers down her spine.

Yet, amidst the trepidation, a glimmer of hope illuminated Ava's heart. She envisioned herself strolling through the sun-kissed campus, forging new friendships beneath the swaying palm trees, and striving for excellence in the pool. The potential for growth and fulfilment at Mission Bay was palpable, if only she could summon the courage to embrace this new chapter.

Contemplating her future, Ava couldn't shake the bittersweet pang in her chest. The prospect of parting ways with Andi after years of shared laughter, tears, and love loomed large. Their bond had weathered storms of judgment, moments of loss, and the winds of change. Yet, as daunting as the distance seemed, Ava found solace in the unwavering strength of their connection.

With resolve in her heart, Ava concluded her application with a final flourish of keystrokes before clicking 'submit'. As the application disappeared into the digital abyss, she gently shut her laptop, wearing a serene smile tinged with determination. Though the road ahead was uncertain, she faced it head-on, bolstered by the unshakeable truth that Andi's love would endure any distance, anchoring her amidst the winds of change.

CHAPTER SEVEN
Happy Birthday

THE HEAVENLY SMELL of chocolate chip pancakes wafting upstairs, woke me up on the morning of my 18th birthday. My mom always went all out making my favourite breakfast foods on my birthday. Throwing back the covers, I jumped out of bed, eager to start celebrating.

Downstairs, our cosy kitchen was decorated with balloons and streamers. "Happy Birthday sweetheart!" Mom greeted me with a huge hug. My dad smiled proudly over his newspaper. "Happy Birthday Angel… our little girl is all grown up now," he said, making me roll my eyes.

After stuffing myself on pancakes, the doorbell rang. I opened it to find Mateo on the front porch grinning from ear to ear. "Happy Birthday dude!" he exclaimed. Wrapping his arms tightly around me, he enveloped me in a warm and affectionate birthday embrace, filling the air with joy. His gesture spoke volumes about his excitement for celebrating this special day with me, radiating pure happiness and gratitude. "Dude, what are you waiting for, let's get this party started!"

I spent the morning laughing and chatting with Mateo as we played video games in the basement like old times. Around noon, the doorbell interrupted us. This time it was my Ava. "Happy Birthday beautiful!" she said, throwing her arms around me. I breathed in the sweet coconut scent of her hair, so happy to have her over.

My mom prepared sandwiches and fruit for us, and the three of us settled down outside on the back patio to enjoy a picnic lunch. The warm June sun felt like the perfect birthday gift after a long Michigan winter. Mateo entertained us with tales of past summer adventures while we ate.

My parents surprised me in the afternoon by taking us all out for a boat ride on the lake. We blasted music and danced around the deck, laughing as we tried not to get knocked over by the waves. The wind whipped through my hair as I leaned over the railing, smiling up at the blue sky.

Back on shore, we built a bonfire down by the beach as the sun began to set. Mateo taught us how to roast the perfect marshmallow for s'mores. I cuddled up next to Ava on a blanket, wishing I could freeze this moment in time. Fireflies blinked in the dusk as we laughed and talked late into the evening.

Around 7 pm, my parents brought out an enormous chocolate cake dotted with candles. My friends sang an enthusiastic, off-key rendition of Happy Birthday. I made a wish — for many more adventures together in our last year before college - and blew out the candles to cheers and applause.

Ava shyly handed me a small wrapped box as we dug into the cake. "It's not much, but I hope you like it," she said. I tore open the paper wrapping to reveal a silver compass on a delicate chain. "It's so you can always find your way back to me," she explained. I hugged her tight, before fastening it around my neck.

Mateo's birthday present turned out to be concert tickets, wrapped up in a mass of newspaper and stuffed into a box, something only Mateo would do. The tickets were to see my favourite indie band later that summer. "I figured we could road trip together and make it a weekend to remember," he said with a smile. I high-fived him excitedly.

After the cake, we gathered around the bonfire again. My dad brought out his guitar, plucking softly as we sang along under the starry sky. I wished we could stay in this perfect moment forever.

Around 10 pm, my parents said goodnight and headed home. The three of us stayed up late talking and laughing about old memories. We promised we'd stay friends no matter what changes life brought after graduation.

Around midnight we decided to call it a night, and put out the fire before climbing into Mateo's car. Our first order of business was to drop off Ava before proceeding to my home. Outside Ava's place, Mateo with a mischievous smile, turned towards me and playfully winked, silently encouraging me to walk her to the door. As the soft light from the front porch enveloped us, I held her close, wrapping my arms around her and silently yearning for the passage of time to halt. Before kissing her goodnight, I whispered in her ear, "Thanks for the best birthday ever".

Ava kissed me softly. "I'm so lucky I get to spend them with you," she said. With a final birthday hug, I watched her slip inside.

Mateo cranked up the radio as we drove through the quiet streets back to my house. "Eighteen, dude! We're officially adults," he whooped. I laughed. "Not sure I'm ready for that yet," I admitted.

He punched my shoulder. "Don't worry. We've still got one more year of fun ahead of us, and I promise you, the adventures are only just beginning."

Gracing the driveway of my home, I paused and gazed upward at the celestial expanse, a smile playing upon my lips. Immersed in a profound sense of contentment, I wondered how life could get any better.

As Mateo pulled away, I crept back inside and up to my room, carefully placing Ava's compass on my nightstand. My birthday wish played over in my head. No matter what new experiences awaited, I knew that Ava and Mateo would remain by my side.

The following day, Ava came around to visit.

We spent the day bundled under quilts exploring sleepy beach towns along the coast of Lake Michigan, which were still frozen with ice while blasting alternative music records in my room. We reminisced about the times when conversation flowed effortlessly between us and we never ran out of things to say to each other.

But all good things come to an end, and saying goodbye to Ava still bore a fierce sting. I'll never forget standing in the grey late afternoon drizzle, watching as the taillights of Ava's car faded down our dirt road. At least this time it wasn't our final farewell; we still had a short time together.

CHAPTER EIGHT

Senior Year

THE END OF junior year arrived much too quickly. As other students eagerly awaited summer vacation, a bittersweet weight hung over Ava and me. In just a few short weeks, Ava would be moving back to California with her dad for her senior year.

Despite the ticking clock, we managed to fully immerse ourselves in the limited time we had together. We indulged in marathon movie nights, ventured out for late-night milkshakes, and committed every detail of each other's faces to memory. Most importantly, we relished in the warmth and comfort of our long, tight embraces, appreciating how perfectly we fit together. Given the undeniable sense of pain and the constant reminder of our limited time together, I made it a point to dedicate myself consciously to being with Ava at every opportunity, ensuring that we made the most of our fleeting days.

The night before Ava's flight, we climbed onto my rooftop with a blanket and snacks. She was uncharacteristically quite as we gazed up at the glittering summer stars. I knew she was likely feeling some of the same swirl of mixed emotions as I was—excitement at seeing old friends, guilt for leaving me, fear of jumping into life alone so far away.

I reached over to give her hand a gentle squeeze. "California won't know what hit them when Ava Wave arrives," I said, attempting to lighten the mood.

She smiled half-heartedly, fiddling with her moon pendant necklace. "I just can't believe I'm actually leaving you and this place. We always spoke about taking on senior year together."

My throat tightened at the quiver in her voice. "I know. But we'll stay in touch no matter what, right? FaceTime every week to swap senior year survival tips and virtual study sessions. I'm sure it will fly by."

Ava just nodded silently and rested her head on my shoulder. We stayed like that for a long time, staring up at the glittering stars as if memorising the summer constellations. Tomorrow a new season of life would begin, but tonight we had the magic of this quiet rooftop and each other.

Driving Ava to the airport the following morning was the most challenging task I've ever undertaken. With our fingers intertwined, we sat in silence, the weight of impending separation heavy upon us. Each passing mile felt like a countdown to the inevitable moment when we would have to part ways. The quiet of the car was punctuated only by the soft hum of the engine, a stark contrast to the whirlwind of emotions raging within us. As we approached the terminal, the reality of saying goodbye loomed larger, casting a shadow over our shared moments of love and laughter. We sat in silence gazing into each other's tear filled eyes.

With a squeeze of our entwined fingers, we silently drew closer to each other and embraced with a kiss.

Inside the airport, Ava clung to me tightly. Our lips met in a final farewell embrace before she disappeared down the boarding tunnel. As she was about to disappear from sight, she consciously turned to savour that one last look. Twenty minutes passed, and I watched her plane soar into the sky, carrying the love of my life off to new adventures.

Saying goodbye never got easier. But the love forged from all we'd weathered together these past years could transcend any distance. I knew her vivid spirit would continue guiding me from sunny California, just like always.

Despite the bittersweet ache, a faint smile crossed my face as the plane disappeared across the horizon. I clung to the memories we shared and the hope of a future together, finding comfort in the promise that someday, some where our paths might intertwine again. But for now, that was enough.

A brisk autumn breeze swirled the first fallen leaves around my feet as I walked up to school on the first day of senior year. With Ava not at my side I felt lost and alone, but it was still exciting and hard to believe this was the first day of my final year of high school. Part of me couldn't wait to graduate and finally move on to college. But another part knew I'd really miss the familiarity of these hallways.

I spotted Mateo waiting by my locker, his signature sunshiny smile in place. He gave me a quick hug. "Dude, today marks the start of our final year in high school, and I am thrilled to have you by my side on this journey."

I rolled my eyes but had to laugh at his dramatic proclamation. The same enthusiastic Mateo, as always. Just seeing his friendly face helped settle the nervous flutters in my stomach. At least I was no longer alone, and we'd tackle this monumental milestone year together.

The first few weeks passed in a blur of syllabi reviews, club sign-ups, and football games under the Friday night lights. Mateo dragged me along to help build colourful floats for the homecoming parade until we were both covered head to toe in glitter and crepe paper scraps.

As the tension mounted, leading up to the game of the season against our biggest competitors..., the drum majorette showcased her talent by expertly directing the halftime marching band performance. Demonstrating controlled enthusiasm, she confidently brandished her baton and sported a tall feathered hat, tilted at a slight angle, adding to her captivating presence. Witnessing Mateo's victorious moment, I couldn't help but cheer proudly as he threw the winning touchdown pass.

Mateo and I decided on a bold whim to attend the homecoming dance together just for fun. I borrowed my dad's old Beatles records to practise my terrible outdated dance moves and begged my mom to help pick out a semi-stylish outfit.

On the night of the homecoming dance, Mateo pulled up outside my house, corsage box in hand. He arrived at the front door, looking effortlessly handsome in his suit. Being the entertainer he is, Mateo pinned the flower to my wrist with a dramatic flourish.

At the festively decorated gym, we spent hours giggling hysterically as we badly recreated every cheesy retro dance trend. For a slow song, Mateo insisted we waltz goofily across the entire dance floor, ignoring the amused looks from our classmates.

Out of breath and cheeks aching from smiling, Mateo twirled me under the neon lights, realising I wouldn't trade these dorky high school memories for anything.

Before either of us had time to worry about the looming future, college application season crashed over us in full force. We spent hours in the library agonising over admission essays and proofreading each other's work.

I stayed up way too late perfecting my writing supplement for the University of Michigan, knowing it was a long shot dream but having to try, anyway. When I got accepted to their honours English program in December, Mateo decorated my locker with balloons and a handmade congratulations banner.

The news of my acceptance filled me with excitement, and I was unable to contain my enthusiasm. I eagerly looked forward to FaceTiming Ava so that I could share the incredible news with her. The demanding nature of senior year had absorbed the majority of our time, making our conversations a delightful reunion as we spoke animatedly until the early hours of the morning. During our exchange, we not only celebrated my achievement but also took the opportunity to catch up on the myriad of experiences and adventures that had unfolded in our lives, cherishing the memories and shared laughter.

Mateo encouraged me to squeeze in the occasional study break to attend football playoffs to destress. Ava and I would FaceTime each other on a regular basis and spend hours binge-watching cheesy holiday movies well past midnight, providing the perfect mindless escape from scholastic pressure. No matter how chaotic life got though, I knew I could always count on Ava's quirky humour and fierce virtual hugs to lift me on those tough days.

Embracing the freedom of the upcoming

winter break, Ava and I found ourselves rejoicing in the triumph of successfully navigating yet another arduous college application season. With a shared sense of accomplishment, we resolved to cap off the season with a memorable holiday adventure. After much deliberation and spirited discussions, we excitedly settled on embarking on a road trip north to explore the enchanting holiday light display in Michigan's little Bavaria - Frankenmuth—a picturesque Bavarian-themed town renowned for its festive charm.

The day of our adventure dawned and anticipation bubbled within me as I made my way to the airport to fetch Ava. Arriving early at our designated meeting point outside of arrivals, I couldn't help but feel a mixture of excitement and nostalgia, recalling the countless shared experiences that had solidified our relationship. Anticipating Ava's imminent arrival with excitement, I envisioned the upcoming road trip not merely as a venture to behold the mesmerising holiday lights, but also as a jubilant celebration of the enduring love we shared, the laughter that echoed through our moments, and the collective joy derived from overcoming challenges as a united front. In my mind's eye, I could picture the miles unfolding before us as a canvas, each stretch of the journey painting vivid strokes of shared experiences and treasured memories.

This impending adventure was set to become a testament to the strength of our bond as we embraced the festive season. Our companionship would turn every twist and turn, on the road into a memorable part of our shared story.

We piled into my snow-dusted car on Christmas Eve as flurries swirled outside the foggy windows. Ava grabbed shotgun privilege and immediately started blasting her offbeat indie playlist. I just laughed and shook my head when weird pan flute solos or heavy bass drops emerged unexpectedly from the speakers.

The wintery landscape rushed by outside as we sang loudly, no doubt off-key. We snacked on homemade sugar cookies and sipped thermoses of hot chocolate to stay warm. By the time we pulled into the glowing wonderland that was Frankenmuth, peppermint chocolate bliss warmed me from the inside out.

Millions of colourful bulbs covered every inch of the quaint old German buildings. We oohed and aahed at the dazzling light displays, snapping selfies with giant nutcracker statues and even getting pulled over by a police horse decked out in bells jingling along Main Street.

Bundled under the twinkling lights strung between shops, everything felt downright magical. Like we'd stepped through our own personal Christmas card into a Snow globe world. The magic of the season sparkled in Ava's eyes as she munched chocolate-covered pretzels and waved at carollers. I wished we could freeze this time and just exist in the holiday spell forever.

After New Year's, the enchantment of the festive season faded, and the realities of the real world loomed ahead. Ava returned to San Diego, and January was filled with student activities for those who had already been accepted, including campus tours of the top colleges.

As I strolled through the lively Diag in Michigan, I couldn't help but feel a sense of disbelief as I laid eyes on the iconic buildings I had fantasised about for years.

Ava and I spent long FaceTime calls debating the pros and cons of big universities versus small liberal arts schools. She was interested in studying music education while I leaned towards English and creative writing. We gently nudged each other to keep an open mind about unexpected paths that could lead to new growth.

As February rolled in, so did both acceptance and rejection letters, serving only to amplify the impending separation, making it feel even more real for both of us. As much as I knew spreading our wings at different colleges was important, actually picturing campus life without my love at my side felt just wrong.

One unusually warm evening, Mateo and I slipped away to the vacant football bleachers and cracked open a bottle of fizzy apple cider that I'd swiped from my fridge. Crickets chirped softly as we passed the drink back and forth, while FaceTiming Ava infused the surrounding air with a blend of nostalgia and melancholy.

"It's hitting me that this is all ending—like, actually ending for real," Ava murmured after a long silence. "The past few years have been an absolute whirlwind of excitement and unpredictability, and we have been fortunate enough to experience it all together. Makes me scared to start over alone somewhere new."

"I know what you mean. I'm freaking terrified of leaving home too." I muttered, staring up at the starry indigo sky, hoping that the universe might beam down some wisdom. "But just think—if your dad had not moved here for work, we'd never have met each other in the first place. Maybe getting thrown into the unknown will end up being amazing."

Ava's lips quirked up thoughtfully. "You and your relentless silver linings. At least I know my best friend's optimism can survive anywhere, even if I have panic spirals."

"Hey right back atcha," I chuckled. "Your courage could inspire anyone to embrace life's surprises."

A comfortable silence enveloped us, extending into the tranquil night sky above Michigan, where I found myself lost in its myriad of twinkling stars. Meanwhile, Ava's gaze was fixated on the luminous glow of the San Diego skyline, each flicker a beacon of possibility illuminating our paths forward. As we basked in the serenity of the moment, our thoughts drifted to the future, a realm teeming with untold mysteries and the promise of dreams realised.

In the midst of this anticipation, I cherished the simple joy of sharing this stolen moment with Ava, connecting through the digital pixels of a FaceTime call. It was in these seemingly mundane exchanges that the essence of our bond thrived, each pixel carrying the weight of our shared experiences and aspirations. In this fleeting instant, I found contentment, knowing that amidst the uncertainties of tomorrow, I had the comfort of Ava's presence to guide me through.

CHAPTER NINE
Prom Night

I STOOD IN front of the full-length mirror, barely recognising the glammed-up girl staring back at me. The lavender chiffon dress hugged my graceful frame, the asymmetric hem showing off my toned legs. Ivory heels added height to my petite stature. My usually straight blonde hair fell in soft curls, pinned back on one side by a shimmering crystal barrette.

Though I felt beautiful, a pang of sadness lingered in my heart. In years past, I had always imagined attending prom with Ava. But with Ava moving to San Diego after junior year, that dream would remain just that — a dream.

Pushing the melancholy aside, I reminded myself how lucky I was to be going with Mateo. When I shyly asked him if he'd be my prom date, his serene smile and immediate "yes!" had relieved my anxiety.

The honk of a car horn outside announced the arrival of Mateo, right on time. With a spritz of floral perfume and one last peak in the mirror, I grabbed my glittery clutch and headed downstairs.

"Wow, you look amazing dude!" gushed Mateo as I slid into the limo's plush backseat. He looked sharp in a sleek black tuxedo, his dark hair neatly styled. "Ava's going to faint when she sees pictures of you."

I grinned, comforted by his kindness.

Knowing Ava, she would be video-calling all night, eager for glimpses of the magical event. It wouldn't be the same as having Ava there in person, but I would appreciate having her along virtually.

As the limo cruised through suburban streets draped in twilight, I chatted with Mateo, glad for his laid-back presence. Though we had never been more than just friends, he had effortlessly agreed to be my prom date, knowing how much it meant to me.

As we pulled up to the venue, I gasped at the sight of the usually drab school gym that had been transformed into an underwater wonderland. Mounds of silver tulle and swaths of glittering blue fabric disguised the space, while strings of twinkling lights mimicked stars.

Joining the elegantly dressed crowd filing inside, I couldn't suppress my delight. A live band played energetic hits, classmates danced enthusiastically, and delicious smells wafted from the buffet tables.

Mateo escorted me through the photo station, where we posed and laughed together. He then whisked me onto the dance floor, spinning me around with playful grace. I let the music transport me, losing myself in the energy and motion. For the first time since Ava had left, my sadness melted away.

As a slow song began, Mateo gently pulled me

into a swaying embrace. "I know I'm not Ava," he said sincerely, "but I hope I'm doing okay as your stand-in prom date."

I smiled up at him. "You're the perfect prom date. Thank you for doing this, Mateo."

The night flew by in a swirl of dancing, talking, and laughter. When the final song played, I felt aglow with joy. As the lights came on, I hugged Mateo tightly. "I'll never forget this night. Thank you for making it so special."

Riding home in the limo afterward, we relived every magical moment. Ava had surprised me by not calling once during the evening. She chose not to interrupt the festivities and allowed me to fully immerse myself in the company of Mateo. The anticipation I felt was almost overpowering as I eagerly awaited the opportunity to video chat with her and share the indescribable experience of prom night. While it may not have unfolded exactly as I had imagined, it somehow managed to surpass all of my expectations.

Later, lying in bed with my laptop, Ava's smiling face filled the screen. "It looked like you had the night of your life," said Ava.

"Oh yes, it was pretty unforgettable. But how about next time you be the one in the purple dress dancing with me all night?"

Ava laughed, her eyes tender. "Deal. After all,

we have the rest of our lives to make up for missed prom nights."

I grinned, as my heart began to swell. The miles between us seemed to disappear. Gazing at my beloved Ava, I knew that someday, no distance would separate us again. Tonight had been magical, but our own shared dance was still to come.

CHAPTER TEN

Graduation

SENIOR YEAR WAS over and the big day I'd been waiting for my whole life had arrived. In just a few hours, I'd be walking across that stage and receiving my high school diploma.

It was guaranteed to be an emotional day. I felt proud of all I had accomplished these past four years. And though part of me was sad that this chapter in my life was ending, I knew an exciting new one was about to begin.

I wished with all my heart that Ava could be here today. But the distance between Michigan and California was too great to expect Ava to make the trip. We would have to settle for video chatting after the ceremony. Still, I missed Ava fiercely. Senior year would have been far tougher without her daily calls and texts.

"Andi, time to go," called mom. With one last peak in the mirror, I headed downstairs, cap and gown in hand. The entire drive to school, I gazed out the window, nostalgia washing over me. How many times had I made this trip with Ava chattering beside me? Though months had passed, I still expected to see Ava's smile lighting up the passenger seat.

At last, we pulled into the crowded parking lot. I joined my classmates, hugs and laughter everywhere. It was bittersweet, but joyous too, this final gathering together. Hand in hand, we walked into the gym to line up, ready to enter the auditorium.

As the strains of the graduation march filled the air, I joined the procession with my classmates, a wide grin spreading across my face as I scanned the audience, teeming with eager family and friends. The multitude of faces blurred into a kaleidoscope of emotions until, in a moment of disbelief, I caught sight of her—could it truly be? I dismissed the notion as a trick of the mind, blinking hard to clear my vision before tentatively glancing back. Yet there she was once more, her radiant smile cutting through the crowd.

I nearly stumbled in shock. What was Ava doing here? Our eyes met and Ava waved eagerly. I waved back, overjoyed tears stinging my eyes. After months apart, Ava had actually flown across the country to surprise me today!

Somehow I kept my composure during the long ceremony. I managed to walk steadily across the stage when my name was called, even as my gaze immediately found Ava cheering wildly in the stands. Then finally, it was over. Caps flew as the new graduates celebrated.

Pushing through the crowd, I flew into Ava's arms. "You're here, you're really here!" I cried.

Ava squeezed me tight. "I couldn't miss your big day! I took a red eye and got in this morning. But I didn't want to ruin the surprise!"

I could hardly speak through the tears. Having Ava here meant everything to me. All these months of missing her, and now here she was, on the most important day of my life. It was the best graduation gift I could have imagined.

The remainder of the day drifted by in a blissful blur — filled with countless hugs, family photos, and a delightful dinner out to mark the occasion. As the hours ticked by, fatigue mingled with exhilaration, culminating in a moment of tranquillity as Ava and I slipped away to the backyard. There, under the mesmerising glow of the Michigan starlight galaxy, we stood hand in hand, lost in its celestial beauty.

"I can't believe that high school's over," I marvelled. "It went by so fast."

"But you made the most of every minute," said Ava. "You have so much to look back on."

I nodded, gratitude welling within me. I turned to Ava, love shining in my eyes. "Having you here today, it's been absolutely perfect. I don't know how I'll ever thank you enough."

"Just seeing your smile today was all the thanks I'll ever need," she said tenderly. "I wouldn't have missed this for the world."

A gentle squeeze of Ava's hand offered solace amid the boundless expanse of the starry sky overhead. The celestial spectacle above us seemed to waltz in perfect harmony with our bond, each shimmering star a testament to the enchantment of the present moment. Holding her hand, I felt an overwhelming sense of belonging and awe, as though we were two wanderers charting our course through the universe, intertwined in its vast tapestry.

Beneath the twinkling stars, I found myself drawn into the depths of Ava's captivating sea-green eyes, where emotions swirled like galaxies yet to be explored. Time appeared to stand still as we engaged in a silent dialogue, our hearts echoing sentiments too profound for words.

As my eyes descended to the soft curve of her lips, I sensed a magnetic force tugging at the very essence of my being, compelling me to lean in closer. It was a sensation akin to the gravitational dance of stars in the vast cosmos, an irresistible pull that defied rational explanation. In that singular, fleeting moment, the boundaries of time and space blurred into obscurity, leaving behind only the raw intensity of our shared connection.

The world around us faded into insignificance as our souls converged, merging in a symphony of passion and desire. It was as though the universe itself held its breath, a silent witness to the profound union unfolding beneath the canopy of stars. And as our lips finally met in a fervent embrace, it was as if the very fabric of reality bowed in reverence, affirming the undeniable power of our love amidst the cosmic expanse. Each tender caress echoed through the cosmos, weaving our story into the tapestry of eternity with an intensity that resonated far beyond the boundaries of time and space.

***

Our unbreakable bond had weathered the storms of senior year across miles and time zones. Now, on the other side, College awaited us, full of promise and adventure. I couldn't help but feel overwhelmed with all the joy we had shared so far. With Ava, every day was a gift. And the next chapter of our lives was just beginning.

OTHER BOOKS BY AUTHOR

Ocean of Chance

Elsa

SHARE YOUR EXPERIENCE

Dear Esteemed Reader,

I am thrilled to extend my deepest gratitude to you for selecting my book from the vast array of options available. Your decision to embark on this literary journey fills my heart with profound appreciation and excitement.

As you immerse yourself in the pages of this book, I hope you find yourself transported into the world I've crafted, drawn to the characters, and engaged by the unfolding narrative. Your experience as a reader is invaluable, and I would be honoured if you could spare a moment to share your thoughts.

Reviews serve as the lifeblood of any writer's career. They offer not only invaluable feedback but also guide other readers in discovering this book amidst the multitude of options available. Whether you choose to share a brief sentiment or provide a detailed analysis, your honest opinion holds immeasurable significance.

If the book resonates with you, I kindly invite you to consider leaving a review on the platform where you acquired or encountered this book. Your support in spreading the word would be immensely appreciated.

Conversely, if the book did not meet your expectations, I welcome your constructive criticism. Such feedback enables me to evolve and improve as a writer, ensuring that future works better align with the desires of my readers.

Once again, I extend my sincerest gratitude for your time, attention, and willingness to embark on this literary voyage with me. Your support fuels my passion for storytelling, and I am deeply grateful for each reader who joins me on this adventure.

Warm regards,

Phoenix Lovegrove

Author of New Girl

www.ingramcontent.com/pod-product-compliance
Lightning Source LLC
Chambersburg PA
CBHW030336160726
47987CB00021B/754